The goalie was racing to get back in front of Clayton, and the fullback was charging him too. But Clayton saw a small opening, and he drove the ball at the net.

The goalie got a leg out and deflected the ball.

But not quite enough!

The ball popped into the corner of the net.

Goal!

Books about the kids from Angel Park:

Angel Park All-Stars

Angel Park Soccer Stars

Psyched!

By Dean Hughes

Illustrated by Dennis Lyall

Bullseye Books • Alfred A. Knopf
New York

A BULLSEYE BOOK PUBLISHED BY ALFRED A. KNOPF, INC.
Copyright © 1992 by Dean Hughes
Cover art copyright © 1992 by Steve Brennan
Interior illustrations copyright © 1992 by Dennis Lyall
ANGEL PARK ALL-STARS characters copyright © 1989
by Alfred A. Knopf, Inc.
ANGEL PARK SOCCER STARS characters copyright © 1991
by Alfred A. Knopf, Inc.

Library of Congress Cataloging-in-Publication Data
Hughes, Dean, 1943–
Psyched! / by Dean Hughes ; illustrated by Dennis Lyall.
p.   cm. — (Angel Park soccer stars ; 4)
Summary: The Angel Park players are so nervous about winning their
upcoming "big game" with Blue Springs that they mess up all over the
place.
ISBN 0-679-82636-X (pbk.) — ISBN 0-679-92636-4 (lib. bdg.)
[1. Soccer—Fiction.] I. Lyall, Dennis, ill. II. Title.
III. Series: Hughes, Dean, 1943– Angel Park soccer stars ; 4.
PZ7.H87312Pan 1992 [Fic]—dc20 91-24715
RL: 2.7
First Bullseye Books edition: April 1992

Manufactured in the United States of America
10 9 8 7 6 5 4 3 2 1

for Diana Hardy

Heads-up Header

Heidi Wells raced to catch up with a pass from the wing. She got to the ball ahead of her defender. But the goalie charged at her, and Heidi had only a split second to get the shot off. She stretched out her leg and whipped the ball at the net. But she lost her balance and fell backward to the grass.

The goalie dove to his left. He punched one hand at the ball, and it bounded high in the air. For a moment Heidi thought she had blown a good chance for a score.

The ball was arching toward her. But she was still on the ground and had no time to jump up and take another shot.

She only had time to react.

The ball was about to come down on top of her when she suddenly thought to throw out her forehead and try a header.

It wasn't much of a shot.

The ball bounced slowly toward the goal. The goalie was trying to scramble to his feet. He flipped around and dove back to his right. Too late!

The ball rolled into the goal.

Heidi couldn't believe it. She had made some lucky shots in her life, but she had never scored sitting down.

She laughed, and for a moment she just sat where she was. And then the next thing she knew, her teammates were piling on top of her.

"Heidi, way to go! Way to go!" They were all screaming.

Now it all sunk in. The Angel Park Pride had finally scored—halfway through the second half. Heidi's team was ahead of the Desert Palm Gila Monsters, 1 to 0.

It had been a tough match all the way. The Desert Palm team was playing better than they had in preseason. Their defense had been almost impossible to break through.

So this was a *huge* goal, and Heidi was thrilled to get it—no matter how! When she got to her feet, she jumped up and threw her fists in the air. She was a tall girl, and a good jumper. She really got high in the air. "*All right!*" she yelled. "Now let's put 'em away!"

The Desert Palm goalie, a muscular guy named Johnny Syme, was standing in front of the goal with his hands on his hips. "You lucked out," he told Heidi.

"Lucked out? You gotta be kidding. I call that shot my 'sitter header.' I make it all the time."

All the Angel Park players laughed.

Syme didn't. He tossed the ball to the referee and then turned and walked away.

Jacob Scott, the other Pride forward and Heidi's good friend, was standing next to Heidi. "Way to use your head," he said, and he laughed.

Heidi gave him a hard stare, and in a voice that seemed serious, she said, "Jacob, I'm starting to realize how *great* a player I am. Not even Pelé could have made goals sitting down."

"Maybe you should play the whole game sitting in the goal area."

"Hey, good idea. Or maybe I could stand on my head and use my—"

"All right! That's enough!"

Heidi turned to see Clayton Lindsay, the all-star English boy on the team. He didn't look pleased.

"Look, it was a lucky goal, and we'll take

it. But we've got to get serious now. We're going to have to play all-out defense and make sure we hang on to this match."

"Don't worry, Clayton," Heidi said. "I have just begun to sit."

"Heidi, I'm serious."

"Oh, Clayton, you're *always* serious. Don't worry. I'll play tough defense. Just as tough as you."

Clayton didn't like that. He turned away. But then he shouted to the rest of the team, "Come on, everyone! We've got to be tough now. Shut off the attack, and let's hang on to this lead. We can't let it slip away from us."

After the score, everyone had seemed happy and relaxed, but Heidi saw the tension set in now. The players were hunched and ready for the kickoff, and they looked deadly serious.

Chris Baca, who was playing right wing for the Pride today, looked around and shouted. "All right, everything's on the line now! Nobody mess up and give away a cheap goal."

Heidi shook her head. What an attitude! She remembered what the coach always said: The best defense was good pressure on attack. A strong attack made the other team think defense.

"Let's go after them!" Heidi shouted. "Let's get another goal and finish them off."

Clayton turned and gave Heidi that glare of his.

Clayton knew—and liked to remind everyone—that a team could think too much about scoring. And that's when a mistake could lead to an easy goal for the other team.

The Gila Monsters were definitely talking *attack* at the other end of the field.

And when they came on the attack, Heidi could see that they had made up their minds to score. They weren't dogging it now. They were running hard, changing speeds, trying to shake their defenders.

Heidi marked a fullback, and she fell back into a defensive position. She had no trouble staying with the big guy. In fact, she cheated off him a little and watched for a chance to help the other defenders.

The Gila Monsters' best player was a quick midfielder named Jimmy Archibald. When he took a drop-off pass in the middle of the field, Heidi saw a chance to set up a trap. She dashed toward him. She and Jacob sandwiched him for a moment.

But Archibald broke through the two defenders and passed off—right to the fullback Heidi had been marking. And the fullback lifted a good pass toward the goal.

A Desert Palm forward, a player named Musselman, went up for a header. But Brian Rohatinsky, Angel Park's sweeper, and Tammy Hill, a fullback, both got up in the air with him. Tammy got her head on the ball and deflected it off to the side.

Clayton picked up the ball and broke upfield. But as the Gila Monsters fell back on defense, he slowed and took his time.

Heidi waited and got in position for a pass. Then she heard Clayton yell, "What were you doing, Heidi? You let your man get wide open."

Heidi didn't answer, but she knew he was right.

Still, she had almost made a steal, and she knew the Pride defense had been back and in good position. If she could have doubled Archibald and stolen the ball, she might have gotten loose for a breakaway. It was a trick that often worked, and something the coach had told the players to do.

In fact, Coach Toscano was yelling at Clayton now. "Go on attack! Pressure them!"

But Clayton was moving slowly, controlling the ball himself. He let the defense settle in before he crossed the halfway line.

And that was the problem. When he tried to pass off to Lian Jie, the other midfielder, a defender was ready. She made a break to the ball and knocked it away.

Just like that, the Gila Monsters were on attack again. And they didn't hesitate. Archibald took a pass and pushed hard up the middle. When Clayton closed in on him, he dropped the ball off to the left wing.

The wing ran along the left touchline, dribbling, and then passed to Musselman.

Musselman tried to go to the goal, but he was cut off. That's when he dropped the ball back to Archibald, and "Arch," as the Gila Monster players called him, looped a pass to Harrison, the right wing.

But Sterling Malone, Angel Park's ace fullback, and Tammy were there. Sterling headed the ball away, but Harrison got it anyway and dropped the ball back to Archibald.

All the pressure was on the Pride defense. Nate Matheson, the Angel Park goalie, was yelling out instructions, and the defense was working very well. But Heidi had the feeling that one of these times a pass was going to get through. The Pride couldn't spend the rest of the game on defense.

She took a chance again.

Archibald dribbled the ball away from the goal and gave his players time to make a move. He angled across the field and watched the goal area to his left.

That's when Heidi left her own mark, sneaked in behind Archibald, and stole the ball. Jacob saw Heidi take the ball, and he broke upfield full blast.

He and Heidi were suddenly off and running, ahead of everyone. Archibald was quick, but not quick enough to make up the ground. Harrison was extremely fast, though, and he raced after them.

Heidi dribbled, hoping she could take the ball all the way. But Harrison, running without the ball, passed her and angled in to try to steal. Heidi passed across to Jacob and kept running.

Harrison had to make his choice. He broke toward Jacob to slow him down and let the defense get back.

Jacob saw Harrison come his way, and he knocked the ball off the side of his foot to Heidi. She was open and clear and only had to beat the goalie. This was it!

But then the whistle blew.

"Offsides," she heard the referee shout.

Heidi pulled up and spun around. "No!" she shouted. "Are you sure?"

The referee came up and put his hand on her shoulder and smiled. "Sorry, but you were ahead of the defender by maybe half a step at the moment the ball was passed."

Heidi nodded. She had to admit, the ref was probably right. At least he was a nice guy about it.

Still, she and Jacob had made a nice run, and she felt good. It was fun to get the pressure back on the Gila Monsters. They would think about it the next time they came on attack.

Clayton walked up to Heidi and said, "You still want to gamble, don't you?"

"Hey, we almost—"

"Yeah, and what if Arch had passed off—with you out of position? You keep it up and we're going to lose our lead."

"Oh, brother!" Heidi said, and she turned and walked away from Clayton.

★ **2** ★

Big Worries

Heidi decided she better not worry Clayton quite so much. She stayed tight on Archibald. She kept him from getting off any serious shots, and she didn't gamble on steals.

But the Gila Monsters kept all the pressure on the Pride defense. As the game got into the closing minutes, the whole team came on hard.

The Pride defense cleared the ball as often as possible. And they used up time whenever they got possession of the ball. But the Gila Monsters' attack never let up. The players knew that time was running out.

Late in the game, Archibald brought the

ball up the middle of the field. Heidi was still marking him close. He passed to his right wing and then cut behind one of his own players. That's when Heidi ran into the player and got knocked down.

Suddenly Archibald was on his own!

He darted toward the goal area, and the wing hit him with a pass. And then, when Sterling came up to guard him, he lifted a little pass in the air toward Musselman.

Tammy got right on Musselman and had him blocked out. He tried to leap for the ball, but he couldn't get his head on it. It bounced off his shoulder and rolled away from the goal.

But Archibald was still charging, and he saw his chance.

He trapped the ball with the inside of his foot, faked a shot, and then broke forward. Tammy and Sterling were closing in from the sides. Heidi was trying to catch up from behind. But Archibald had a slice of space, and he blasted a hard shot.

Heidi's breath caught. The ball was heading for the . . .

But Nate was in the right position.

The ball hit Nate square in the chest and bounced in front of him.

Sterling was on top of the ball quickly, and he tried to drop it back to Nate.

But Archibald wasn't finished yet. He dove at the ball with his leg outstretched, and he tried to knock it past Nate again.

Nate was diving, too.

He got hold of the ball just as Archibald's foot hit it.

Heidi didn't know whether Nate could hang on, but he did. He pulled the ball to his chest and rolled up with it for a moment.

Then Nate leaped up, took a couple of steps, and punted the ball well up the field.

Suddenly the whistle sounded, and the match was over.

The Pride had come within an inch of blowing their lead with just seconds on the clock. Heidi flopped on the grass, exhausted. She looked over at Nate, who was bending over with his hands on his knees. He was too tired to celebrate quite yet.

"That didn't scare me," Heidi said, and she laughed. "What about you?"

Heidi had a funny square sort of smile and a husky laugh. It was hard not to laugh when she did. Nate grinned. "I knew I had it—all the way."

But Clayton didn't think the whole thing was quite so funny. "Heidi, how did you let Archibald get away like that?" he said. It was more an accusation than a question.

Meanwhile, the other Pride players had begun to let it sink in that they had actually won. Tammy and Billy Bacon, a substitute fullback, gave each other a big high-five. Tammy yelled to the other players, "Hey, we could go all the way this year. We're three and one!"

Heidi liked that. Last season had started badly. The Angel Park team had lost most of its early games. So things *were* looking up!

Heidi wanted to be happy, but right now she still had Clayton glaring at her. He acted as though the Pride had lost.

"Clayton, I got knocked down. I don't know what else to tell you."

"You should have cut behind the guy and then picked Archibald up."

"I didn't even see the guy until he knocked into me."

"Well, then, try looking."

Jacob had gone around and slapped hands with some of his teammates, but as he approached Heidi, he heard what Clayton was saying. "Hey, Clayton, come on," he said. "Things like that happen. She was watching Archibald, and she didn't see that guy."

"That's right. And we almost gave up a goal because of it."

"Well, let's see," Jacob said, "I guess you've never made a mistake in your whole life."

"Shut up, jerk," Clayton said, and he walked away.

The Pride players stopped celebrating and looked to see what was happening. Everyone was suddenly quiet.

And they were still quiet when they walked out and slapped hands with the Desert Palm players.

Coach Toscano hadn't heard exactly what

Clayton and Jacob had said, but he knew something was going on. He called the players together.

"Hey, what's the matter, gang?" he said, and he grinned. "We just won. You look like we got beat."

Trenton Daynes said, "Yeah, well, it's Clayton who thinks we lost. It's not good enough for him that we got a shutout. We all have to be *perfect*—like he thinks *he* is."

"Hey, Trenton," the coach said, "let's not talk that way."

"It's true, Coach," Henry White said. He usually didn't have a lot to say, but he sounded upset now. "Clayton was all over Heidi. I guess he's never gotten knocked down before."

"You guys don't know what you're talking about!" Clayton shouted.

Coach Toscano held his hands up. "Wait! Now everyone stop yelling." He waited a few seconds, and then he said, "Now, Clayton, why don't you tell me what this is all about."

"We had the game won. All we had to do was play smart. But Heidi kept taking chances. Maybe she couldn't help getting knocked down there at the end, but she didn't have to drop off her man all the time and go for steals."

"What do you say to that, Heidi?" the coach asked. He was smiling, as though he already knew what Heidi's answer would be.

"You always tell us not to get too careful, to keep the pressure on their defense. I thought if I could steal, and we could score, we'd have them. It was a good time to try to catch them, when they had no one back on defense."

"Fine," Clayton said. "If you get a clean steal. But you were letting Arch get free. And that's taking too big a chance!"

"Wait a minute," Coach Toscano said. "Don't start shouting again." He smiled. "Heidi is right. We should never stop attacking. But Clayton has a good point. Some gambles aren't worth taking, especially when we have a lead late in the match."

"Okay," Heidi said. "I'll be more careful next time."

But the coach didn't seem happy with that. "Heidi, remember, it's always a close judgment. I still say *attack*. Don't get careful. That steal you made might have gotten us a goal if we hadn't gotten the offside call."

Heidi understood. She knew that sometimes she did take big chances. But she had won some games that way. She would just have to watch that she didn't overdo it.

Still, as far as she was concerned, the whole matter was settled. She just hoped that Clayton would calm down.

"Clayton," the coach was now saying, "you know this game well. But if a team doesn't play together, nothing good is going to happen. Shouting at your teammates really isn't going to do anyone any good."

"I know, Coach. I'm sorry." He sort of glanced at Heidi. Maybe that was his way of apologizing.

"Okay, fine," Coach Toscano said. "Let's just try—"

"Coach?"

"Yes, Clayton."

"We've got a chance to win it all this year.

But if we're going to beat the Springers, we're going to have to be at our *best*. We can't be letting players run free."

"All right, Clayton. You've already made your point. And I think Heidi understands. But let me remind you of something. We play Cactus Hills on Thursday before we play the Springers. Let's not look past them."

"That's right," Jared Trajillo said. He was starting to be more vocal now that the coach was training him to be a goalie. "We just *can't* lose to them. They stink!"

"Don't worry. We can beat *those guys*," Billy said.

But no one seemed to like that. Henry was the first to say, "They're not pushovers. They've lost some games, but they can play. We're going to have to be tough."

Everyone started talking at once, and now all the players seemed to have Henry's attitude. The team was on its way now, but they knew they had to stay tough against Cactus Hills.

Clayton finally spoke above the rest. "Coach, I didn't mean that we should look past anyone. We can't lose *any* matches. But we *must* beat the Springers."

For the first time, Nate spoke up. "That's right," he said. "We can go all the way. But we can't let down for a second. We've got to win every single match now. I think maybe *we* can beat the Springers, but I don't know if anyone else can."

Coach Toscano threw up his hands again. "Wait a minute, kids. Let's not look at the whole season. Let's just take one game at a time and play hard. But don't start telling yourself you have to win every match."

"But we *do* have to win them all, Coach," Clayton said.

Nate was nodding his head. And most everyone else was agreeing. Heidi didn't like what she was seeing. She wanted to win as much as anyone, but she didn't like the pressure the players were putting on themselves. All this "win-win" talk was crazy!

Still, she seemed to be the only one who felt that way—except for Coach Toscano. Even Jacob was telling Nate, "There's no way we can let Cactus Hills beat us. If we do that, we're finished."

Heidi couldn't believe it. Everyone sounded so uptight. And that wasn't going to do the team one bit of good.

★ 3 ★

The Race Is On

On Tuesday night the team practiced. Coach Toscano tried hard to have some fun. He divided the players into teams of three, and he had them compete with one another on some passing drills. He had a bag of candy bars with him, and he tossed some to the winners of each little match. And he joked with all the players, calling them nicknames when they scored.

Heidi could see that Coach Toscano was trying to get the players to enjoy themselves—and one another.

And it worked.

But practice was no sooner over before Clayton and Nate started talking about how important it was that the Pride *not* lose to the Cactus Hills Racers.

Heidi watched everyone get quiet. "Man, we just *can't* let that happen," Adam Snarr said. He didn't play a lot, but he liked to win as much as anyone. "We've got to play a lot better on Thursday."

Heidi hated to see this stuff get started again. "Yeah, if we lost, the sun probably wouldn't come up the next morning," she said. "Or even if it did, we'd have to go around with long faces for the rest of our lives."

But that was the wrong thing to say. A lot of the players turned to look at her, and she knew what they were thinking.

Nate was the one who said it. "Come on, Heidi. Don't you even care if we lose?"

"Sure I do. So let's win. But let's not stand around talking about how awful it would be if we lost. What kind of attitude is that?"

"It's just plain true," Clayton said as he walked away.

Heidi rolled her eyes. Then she pulled Nate aside. Jacob was there, too.

"For crying out loud, Nate," she said. "You

guys are getting everyone worried. We're not going to play our best that way."

"We're not going to play our best if we don't take the Racers seriously either. We've got to have our heads in the game."

"Okay, okay. Take mine. You can use it for a soccer ball."

"Is that supposed to be funny or something?"

"Hey, whoa!" Jacob said. "Don't you two start getting on each other now."

Nate and Heidi had been best friends for a long time. Heidi didn't want any bad feelings either. "Hey, I'm not getting on anyone," she said. "But Nate takes things too seriously. He knows that."

She looked straight at Nate. "Just loosen up a little. Let's play hard and beat 'em—and quit worrying so much."

"Maybe I'm too serious sometimes," Nate said. "But your trouble, Heidi, is that you're not serious enough."

Now it was Nate who was walking away. "Hey, wait," she said. But Nate kept right on walking. Heidi figured she had better lay off for now and talk to Nate later. He never stayed mad.

So Heidi walked home with Jacob. He told her that maybe she should be a little more careful about the things she said. She didn't want everyone to think she didn't care.

"I'll let my playing speak for itself," she told him, and that's what she made up her mind to do on Thursday.

But when the team took the field that day, she didn't like what she saw. Jimmy Gerstein, the Racers' smart-mouthed forward, started in as usual. He told the Angel Park players that he was going to show them up today.

And instead of laughing and talking it up with one another, the Pride players were looking grim. They yelled back and forth, but half the comments were like Clayton's: "All right. Let's not let them get any cheap scores."

Heidi yelled, "Let's get after 'em. Let's get some early goals."

"Yeah!" some of the players yelled, but not with the excitement and confidence Heidi wanted to hear.

And not long after the kickoff, the Pride had some bad luck that didn't help at all.

The Pride got control of the ball early, and Clayton passed in deep to Jacob in the goal area. Jacob dropped off a nice pass to Henry, who was coming in from the wing.

Henry seemed to have a perfect shot, but the grass had been watered that morning, and it was still wet in places. He slipped just as he was about to fire. He got a shot off, but it was weak, and the goalie ran over and knocked the ball away.

But that was great luck compared to what happened a couple of minutes later.

The Pride was having no problem in the middle of the field. Clayton and Lian were dominating the Racers' midfielders. And most of the play was in the Pride's attacking end of the field.

But the Racers finally worked the ball up the field and got it to Gerstein. Sterling marked him well and then moved in for a tackle. He knocked the ball away, and Jared chased it down.

The Pride players yelled, "Attack!" and they took off upfield. But Jared tried to pass off to Chris Baca, and Gerstein cut between them and stole the pass back.

Sterling covered Gerstein, and the defense began to fall back. Gerstein tried to strike quickly while he had the advantage. He took a hard shot. But Sterling got a foot out and blocked it.

The ball bounded off Sterling's foot in the direction of the goal. Nate took a couple of steps forward and was in a good position. But the ball took a high bounce.

He tried to step toward the ball, but his foot slipped on a wet spot, and he went down on one knee.

The ball still had some speed on it, and it was high in the air. Nate had no time to get up. He reached, but the ball bounced over him and into the net.

It was unbelievable. Nate fell on his face, and Heidi, who had also been trying to get to the ball, dropped to her knees.

"Oh, man! They lucked out!" she told Nate.

He got up and kicked at the grass. "I was afraid something like this was going to happen," he said. "Look at Gerstein. You'd think he just did something great."

Gerstein was still jumping up and down, and he was shouting, "We're going to get you guys today. It's *our* day!"

"Let's forget it," Heidi told him. "We'll get the goal back—right away."

But it didn't happen.

Clayton called out to the players, "That's what happens when we break too fast after stealing the ball. If we had had more people back, the ball wouldn't have gotten through like that."

Heidi thought she saw the team tighten up even more after that.

The players weren't moving out on attack. They were being careful until they moved the ball into the Racers' end of the field. By then the defense was set up and hard to break.

The Racers didn't really threaten to score after that, with the Pride defense staying so tough, but Angel Park wasn't getting many scoring chances either.

Just before the half, however, the Pride finally got a good opening.

Tanya Gardner, who was now playing right wing, made a nice center pass to the goal area. Heidi was blocked out and couldn't get to the ball. A Racer fullback tried to volley it out of the goal area, but he didn't really hit the ball well.

The ball sort of trickled away, and Jacob pounced on it. The middle was jammed, and he had no chance for a shot, but he kicked it over to Henry. Henry dropped it back to Clayton.

Clayton dribbled to his right, and then reversed himself and cut to the left. He passed off to Heidi, but she was marked, and her defender kicked the ball away.

The ball was rolling free in the middle.

Heidi dashed after it.

The Racers' goalie had also seen the danger, and he broke for the ball. He dove just as Heidi got there. She beat him, and she blasted a hard shot at the open net. But she had hurried a little, and her shot was more to the right than she had wanted.

The ball hit the legs of a Racer defender who was breaking in to try to cover the goal. The ball bounced away and rolled to the right of the goal. One of the Racers' fullbacks got to the ball first and cleared it.

And that was that.

If Heidi had been able to get the shot six inches to the left, it would have been an easy goal.

But now it was a big nothing, and the score was still 1 to 0.

And that's what it was when the Pride walked off the field at halftime.

"Not *one thing* has gone right for us today," Nate was complaining.

Clayton was mad enough to chew down the goalposts. "How can we have such lousy luck?" he said. "Gerstein's shot *bounces* in—and Heidi's gets blocked by someone who wasn't even looking."

All the Pride players were talking about the terrible luck when they sat down on the grass.

But Coach Toscano told them, "Hey, kids, luck is a big part of this game. We've outplayed the Racers all the way. Let's just keep it up, and the ball will bounce our way one of these times."

"It better start bouncing for us right away," Clayton said. "If we lose this match, our season is *finished.*"

Coach Toscano was quick to stop that. "Hey, gang," he said, "enough of that. Let's talk about winning, not losing. Let's talk about what we're going to do in the second half."

But Heidi didn't like what she was seeing. The Angel Park players all had their heads down.

★ 4 ★

That's the Way the Ball Bounces

Coach Toscano was finally a little upset with the kids. "All right!" he told them. "Let's just get out there and play the way we did last week. Let's get after them and win this match."

"Yeah," Heidi said. "Let's get *going!*"

And that's what happened. The Pride went out in the second half and played with some spirit. They kept the pressure on up front. And finally something went their way.

Trenton saw a Gerstein pass coming. He stepped in and stole the ball. Then he kicked the ball to Clayton.

Clayton took a couple of slow steps and then, suddenly, turned on the speed and got past his defender. Once he got in the clear, he passed the ball well up the field to Heidi.

Heidi jumped up and let the ball hit her thigh and then drop to the grass. She turned to see that she had some space, and she took advantage of it.

Heidi drove hard toward the goal area and forced a fullback to come up to cover her. Then she kicked a slanting pass over to Jacob. He had dropped back from the goal area a little to get himself clear—and to avoid being offside.

He turned to his right, as though he were going to kick the ball over to Clayton in the middle of the field. But suddenly he spun back and lifted a high pass to Heidi. She had run to the center of the goal area.

Heidi saw the pass coming, but her defender didn't. She beat him into the air, and slammed a header past the goalie and into the top of the net.

Bang! Just like that.

The goal had looked easy. But the Pride had kept good pressure on the defense. Finally they had found the right chance. And they had used it!

Now the score was tied, 1 to 1.

They could do that again, Heidi told herself. They were wearing the Racers down.
Gerstein was cursing and shouting at the rest
of his team. As usual, he was putting all the
blame on everyone but himself.

Now was the right time to go after these
guys.

"Okay," Heidi yelled. "Let's turn up the
heat. Let's get another one, right away!"

Everyone was yelling the same thing. And
for the first time, Clayton looked excited.
"Nice shot!" he told Heidi. "Let's get some
more. Let's put these guys away."

He and Heidi ran back for the kickoff.
Heidi had the feeling that the team was back
together again. Now they just had to keep
that spirit going and they would be all right.

And sure enough, the Pride was soon
coming on hard. They got off several shots
in the next five minutes. But they couldn't
get a good clear opening, and nothing got
into the net.

Still, it was just a matter of time.

Or so it seemed.

The Pride kept taking their shots and not
quite getting a score. But once they came *so
close.* Clayton got the ball at the front of the

goal area and saw a chance to knock the ball home.

But just as he let the shot fly, a fullback came from behind him and stuck out a foot. He only grazed the ball, but Clayton had aimed for the left corner. The partial block pushed the ball outside the goalpost and over the goal line.

And then, on the corner kick that followed, Tanya made a great kick to the corner of the goal. Jacob tried to volley it into the net.

But the goalie gambled and guessed right. He dove into the path of the ball and made a great save.

Gerstein really let the Angel Park players have it each time they came close and missed. "Hey, Jacob, what's the matter?" he yelled. "Is our goalie just too good for you?"

Jacob just walked away from him. But Heidi thought she saw some of the discouragement returning to her teammates' faces. Some of the parents were yelling from the sidelines, "Keep it up. You've just had some tough luck so far."

"Why can't we get a break today?" Jacob mumbled.

Henry shook his head and said, "We should be ahead by three or four goals by now."

And maybe it was that discouragement that began to turn things the wrong way. Not long after Jacob's blocked shot, Gerstein took a throw-in and made a nice move to get past Chris.

He passed off to a midfielder and then took a pass right back. He tried to get past Sterling and got stopped. He passed off to a kid named Gunther, another bigmouth like Gerstein.

But Gunther got doubled, and for a moment he was trapped. Just when he seemed about to lose the ball, he kicked at it and knocked it between the two defenders. He couldn't get to the ball himself, but Gerstein sprinted over and took control.

Gerstein smiled a little, and he looked Sterling in the eye. He dribbled slowly to the left. Then he cut the ball behind his right foot and made a quick reverse move.

But he didn't shake Sterling.

All the same, that's when the luck seemed to turn toward the Racers.

Gerstein tried to put another move on

Sterling. He feinted to the left, then pushed the ball right between Sterling's legs. He hoped to break past Sterling and pick up the ball behind him.

But Sterling stayed tough and didn't get out of position. He spun quickly and controlled the ball before Gerstein could get around him.

Gerstein was frantic to make up for his mistake. He ran right into Sterling, trying to get back to the ball. The boys' legs tangled, and suddenly both were sprawled across the grass. Heidi expected a whistle and a foul on Gerstein.

Sterling must have expected the same thing.

But nothing happened. No whistle sounded.

Gerstein was on top of Sterling. He scrambled up and got back to the ball. And now Gerstein, without anyone to guard him, broke toward the goal.

Clayton was screaming, "Foul! Foul!" But he also raced in to try to stop Gerstein.

At the same moment, Gerstein blasted a sharp pass to Gunther and then looped in a half circle toward the goal. Clayton saw what Gerstein was up to and stayed right with him. When Gunther tried to return the pass to Gerstein, Clayton cut it off.

Almost.

He stopped the pass but he didn't control it, and the ball rolled free in the goal area. That's when a wing seemed to come out of nowhere and *bam!* She knocked the ball home.

Now the Racers were ahead, 2 to 1.

The Racers went crazy. They jumped all over each other.

Clayton was almost as wild. "Whose mark was that?" he kept screaming. "Who let her get loose?"

But no one knew exactly. When Clayton dropped off to cover Gerstein, a lot of switching had had to take place. Sterling had gotten up and raced to Gunther, but that was double coverage. Somehow, no one had picked up the girl on the right wing.

"Whose mark was that?" Clayton screamed again.

"I don't know," Sterling told him. "You switched and so did a lot of us. I guess maybe I should have picked her up. It was just a mix-up. You did what you had to do, and we all tried to do the same."

Clayton was furious, but he must have also

seen that Sterling was right. And so suddenly he spun to the referee. "Why didn't you call that foul?" he screamed. "Gerstein knocked our man flat on his face."

"They got tangled with each other, son. That's what it looked like to me."

"You're crazy. They—"

Suddenly the whistle was blowing. Clayton had himself a red card—just like that.

And that meant Clayton was ordered out of the game and the Pride had to finish with only ten players.

And that meant the match was over, basically.

The Pride played hard. They went all out on attack. But they really needed Clayton in the middle.

And they needed to believe they could do it. Heidi heard everyone talking tough, but she also saw how hesitant they were. "Come on," Nate yelled from the goal. "We gotta pull this out. We just *can't* lose it."

And that's how everyone played, as far as Heidi was concerned—as though they were afraid of losing. They pushed the ball up the field, but they seemed tight and nervous.

Jacob had a chance to get a shot off, but he hesitated a split second too long. He got the shot blocked.

Henry broke into the clear once, but he took his eyes off the ball as he took a pass from Lian. He tried to make a break to the goal before he really had the ball under control. He let it roll away, and the Racers picked it up.

As time was running out, the Pride had one last chance. Tammy got a rebound off a blocked shot, but she tried to get too much power on the ball. She leaned back too far and kicked under the ball. It sailed high over the goal.

When it was all over, Gerstein really rubbed it in. He taunted Clayton on the sidelines until the coach had to grab Clayton to keep him from going after the guy.

But that was the least of the worries for the Angel Park team. They had lost two games now. The Springers and the Kickers had only lost one. Lots of games were still left in the season. But maybe the Pride would *never* catch up.

★ 5 ★

Upside Down

Coach Toscano didn't seem all that upset after the match. He told the players that some days were like that. "We got some bad breaks, but we played very well at times. We just need to get ready for Monday's match."

"What difference does it make?" Clayton blurted out. "We can't win the championship now."

Coach Toscano didn't like that. "Clayton, I've heard enough of that kind of talk!" he said. "Yes, we do have a chance for the championship. But even if we didn't, our job would still be to play the best we can in every match. We aren't giving up just because we lost today."

Clayton kept his mouth shut after that, but the team seemed to take on his gloomy attitude. Heidi heard a couple of the kids saying that the Pride wouldn't have a chance against Blue Springs.

She walked home with Nate and Jacob, and she expected Nate to be feeling the same way. But she was surprised when he said, "Clayton's getting the whole team down. Everyone thinks we're finished now that we lost today."

"Wait a minute!" Heidi said. She came to a stop in the middle of the sidewalk. Jacob and Nate took another step or two and then stopped and looked back at her. "You're the guy who said we absolutely *had* to win to-day."

Nate suddenly thought the sidewalk was more interesting than Heidi's face. "I know. And that's how I felt, too. But now that we lost, we can't tell ourselves the whole season is down the drain. We have to beat the Springers somehow, and then hope we can win the rest of our matches."

"And what if we lose to the Springers? Do we just quit playing?"

"No, Heidi. But you don't know how much I want to win a championship once in my life. If we lose to Blue Springs, I don't see how we could do it."

Heidi started to walk again. She was trying to figure out how to tell Nate what she was thinking. "Nate, it doesn't work to think that way."

"What way?"

"Upside down."

"What?"

"It's like if someone offers you an ice-cream cone, and you say, 'Well, yeah, I'd like one, but it might drip on my shirt, so never mind.' "

"Heidi, that's stupid. I don't even know what you're talking about."

Heidi looked over at Jacob. "Do you get what I'm saying?" she asked.

"Actually, no." Jacob gave her that split-toothed grin of his and sort of shrugged his shoulders.

"Okay, let me put it another way." Now Heidi had to think again. "You want to win the championship, right?"

"Sure," Nate answered.

"Okay. Why?"

"I want to know what it's like to win."

"So you think you're really going to be happy if you win the championship—right?"

"Right."

"So is the best way to get to that wonderful, happy day by being miserable all season because you're afraid you won't get there?"

Nate gave Heidi a strange look, but Jacob seemed to get the idea. "Yeah, that's right, Nate," he said. "We want to win, but we can't spend the whole season afraid we won't. That's no fun."

Heidi added, "What good is a great ending to the season if the season isn't fun?"

"But winning *is* fun," Nate said. "That's all I want to do—win."

"Sure. But you and Clayton are always saying, 'We just *can't* lose.' All that does is make everyone tight. You're the one who just said the team is down. And that's why."

Nate was carrying a soccer ball, and he bounced it on the sidewalk a couple of times as he walked. Heidi could see that he was thinking things over.

"Maybe that's right," he finally said. "I do

think we play worse when everyone starts talking like Clayton. I got into that today."

Heidi stopped suddenly again. "Whoa. Did you hear that?" She spun around and looked, as though she had heard something from behind her.

"What?" Jacob said.

"Is this an echo canyon we're walking in? I think I just heard my own words bouncing back at me."

"Shut up," Nate said, but he was smiling.

Heidi echoed his words back to him: "SHUT UP . . . SHUT UP . . . Shut up."

Then she grabbed the ball out of Nate's hands. "Soccer ball, your master needs a lot of help. He's hearing voices—and repeating what they say. You better watch him pretty closely."

"Okay, okay," Nate said. "But what do we do? No one on the team thinks we've got a chance against Blue Springs. Somehow we've got to get everyone thinking differently before Monday."

As the three walked past a house, they saw an older man sitting on the front porch. "Hey, kids, how did you do today?" he called out.

No one wanted to answer. Finally Heidi said, "We got beat, two to one."

"Oh, no," the man said. "I thought you kids had a good team this year."

"We do," Nate said. "But we had a bad day."

"Better not have any more," the man said, and he laughed.

"We're not planning to," Nate told him.

But Heidi whispered, "See, everyone thinks the same way. 'You better not lose.' That's all people think about."

"Hey, everyone in Angel Park cares about the teams. Sports are about the biggest thing around here."

"I know. But that just makes all the players worry more about losing. They don't want to have to tell people they *failed*."

"So what do we do about it?" Jacob asked.

"I don't know. I'm thinking."

Heidi walked in silence. She still had the feeling that her teammates were looking at things upside down.

Suddenly she stopped again. She stepped onto someone's lawn, bent down, and put her head on the grass. Then she slowly lifted her feet until she was standing on her head.

"What the heck are you doing?" Nate wanted to know. But he was laughing and so was Jacob.

"The world is all upside down, so I'm trying to see it straight."

"Weird," Jacob said. "The girl is weird."

All the same, Heidi was getting an idea as she stood on her head. She dropped her feet to the ground and stood up straight.

"Okay, I've got it. We're going to have a victory party."

"For a loss?" Nate asked.

"No, for a win."

"What win?"

"The win over the Springers."

"Yeah, well, we have to beat them first."

"No, we don't. We'll have the party first, and then we can beat them later."

"Yeah, sure. And what if we lose?"

"Nate, there you go again."

Nate looked very confused, and so did Jacob. But Heidi didn't care. She thought she had just the right idea to get the team back on its feet.

★ 6 ★

Victory Party

That night Heidi called the coach and talked with him about her idea. He thought the party sounded great. He and Heidi agreed to hold it Saturday afternoon—at Heidi's house.

"But Coach," Heidi said, "let's not tell them it's a party. Let's call it a team meeting. They'll be ready for something serious—and then we'll surprise them."

The coach liked that. He and Heidi talked about some things they could do. Coach Toscano said he would order pizza, and he had some videos that would make everyone laugh.

"Okay," Heidi said. "I'll call all the players. And I'll tell them you said it was a required meeting."

"Okay, good. Make it sound very important."

"Don't worry. I know how to do that."

So Heidi hung up the phone and got out her team list. She was all ready to start calling everyone when it hit her: Maybe she ought to check with her parents first.

Heidi's dad was in the family room. He was reading the paper and watching the evening news at the same time. That's what he did every night. Mrs. Wells was there too, but she was only watching the news.

"Mom, Dad," Heidi said as she walked into the room.

Mom looked up and said, "Yes," but Dad kept his nose in the paper and mumbled, "Uh-huh."

"Can we have a party for the soccer team on Saturday?"

"Here?" Mom asked.

"Yeah. But you don't need to do anything. The coach is ordering pizza, and we'll have it out in the backyard."

"Well, yeah," Mom said. "But it might be kind of cool outside."

"It's okay. It'll be warm enough." Then she turned to her dad. "Is that okay with you? I'll mow the lawn."

"Uh-huh."

"Could we also use the pool?"

"Uh-huh."

"Hey, Dad?"

"Yeah."

"We don't have a pool."

He finally looked up. "What?"

"How can we use the pool if we don't have one?"

"Well, if we don't have one, I wouldn't use it."

"No wonder kids call me weird. I think I inherited a sick mind."

Dad grinned and then went back to his paper.

"How come you're having a party in the middle of the season?" Mom asked. Everyone said that Heidi and her mom looked *exactly* alike. They were both tall. They both had four-cornered sort of smiles. And they both had dark hair. But Mom wore hers long, and Heidi's was cut very short.

"It's a victory party," Heidi said.

"After a loss?"

"That's what everyone says, Mom. I can't figure out how people think."

"What?" Mom was staring. She often did that. Heidi could be pretty confusing.

But Dad said—even though Heidi didn't think he had heard a word—"That's a great idea, Heidi. That's what your team needs."

"A victory party after a loss?" Mom asked again.

"Yup," Heidi said.

"Yup," Dad said.

"Will you pay for the pizza then?" Heidi asked.

"No way. You guys lost. What do *you* have to celebrate?"

"How about lending me some money then, and *I'll* pay for the pizza."

"Okay. As long as you don't pay me back."

"I swear. You're both weird," Mom said.

Heidi smiled and walked back to make the phone calls. It was nice to know that Dad understood. At least Dad—and Coach Toscano—knew what she was trying to do.

At practice on Saturday morning Heidi heard the players talking about the Springers and how good they were. No one said, "We don't have a chance," but she knew that's what they were thinking.

When the coach reminded the players about the meeting that afternoon, he made it sound like a big deal. "I want everyone to be there," he told them. "We need to get ready for the game on Monday."

"Are we going to change our attack or something?" Clayton asked.

"Yes. I think you could say that. Just come, and you'll see what I have in mind."

Everything was ready. When the players started showing up that afternoon, Heidi had them go to the backyard. She had set some chairs on the patio. She had them all facing in the same direction—the way she would have set up for a meeting.

And the players seemed to be ready for one. They sat down and they talked some, but they seemed serious.

Once everyone was seated, Coach Toscano stood up in front.

"I'm glad you could come today," he said. "I think we need to make some adjustments before Monday's game."

Coach Toscano almost always smiled, even at serious times. But he wasn't smiling now. The players had never been this quiet before.

"We played a good game on Monday," Coach Toscano said, "and we didn't really play badly on Thursday. What I'm seeing is a team that is capable of beating anyone in the league. Don't you think so?"

Clayton, of course, was quick to answer. "Coach, I think that's right. But we have to play our *very* best to beat the Springers. We can't let down for a single second. Blue Springs has more speed than we do, so we'll have to run harder and get back quicker on defense."

Coach Toscano looked around. "Is that how the rest of you feel?"

No one said anything. The players seemed to accept that Clayton knew more about soccer than anyone else.

"What do you think about that, Heidi?" Coach Toscano asked.

"I think we should celebrate."

"Celebrate what?"

"Celebrate that we're going to *get after* Blue Springs and have a great time. I think we're going to win."

Heidi heard Clayton sort of moan. The coach looked at him. "What's wrong, Clayton?"

"I think it's way too soon to start talking big. Right now we need to talk about some of the mistakes we've been making and see if we can't get them straightened out."

"We worked on that at practice this morning," the coach said. "I thought we looked very good, too."

"Yes, but that was against our own players. The Springers are . . . well . . ."

"Better?"

Clayton didn't want to answer that one. "I'm just saying we can't mess up the way we did on Thursday."

The coach nodded. He looked around at the players, his face long and gloomy. "Well, Clayton makes a very good point," he said. "We have to play our best."

Again he paused and considered, and he looked all around.

Then, suddenly, that huge smile of his broke across his face.

"And that's why I think Heidi is right. Let's forget about the mistakes we *might* make. Let's quit worrying about losing. Let's just get after the Springers on Monday— give it everything we've got—and see what happens. Let's have some fun."

Everyone was staring at the coach as if they weren't quite sure what to think.

But Clayton seemed alarmed. "Coach, don't we need to talk about—"

"No, Clayton. We've talked a lot. And we've practiced. What we need to do now is eat some *pizza!*"

He burst out laughing. And then he added, "Let's have fun now, and on Monday let's go out there and play soccer as though we enjoyed the game. Let's not hear any more talk about how bad it will be if we lose. It's time to celebrate!"

"Gee, Coach," Heidi said, "we just happen to have some pizza. Should I bring it out?"

"Good idea!"

Nate and Jacob were sitting next to her. She asked them to help her, so they followed her into the kitchen. And the celebration began.

Most of the players seemed confused. They were happy about the pizza, but they hardly knew what to think about the idea of celebrating *before* the match.

Still, every time someone tried to talk about strategy or the need to win, Heidi or Coach Toscano would say, "Hey, this is a victory party. Don't talk soccer. Just have fun."

Clayton took the longest to catch on to the spirit of things. "Clayton, this week we went into a match worrying about losing," the coach told him. "We're never going to do that again. This next match we're going in thinking about how much fun it's going to be to win."

"That doesn't mean we'll win, just because we say it," Clayton told him.

"No, it doesn't. But we'll have a lot better chance if we're relaxed and playing all out—and we're not tight."

Clayton nodded, as though he understood.

That's when the coach said, "You've got to be the one to lead the way, Clayton."

Clayton seemed to accept that. He had as much fun as anyone at the victory party. And when he got a chance, he told the team, "Look, everyone, I'm sorry about the way I acted in that last match. Sometimes I just get carried away. I want to win so badly—that's all I can think about. But that isn't going to help us. The coach is right—and so is Heidi. We need to get *psyched,* as you Americans say. But that doesn't mean worried and upset. It means confident—and *intense.* Let's be a pride of *lions!*"

That brought a big cheer from the players.

Heidi liked what she was seeing—a lot of laughing and fun, but no more "we gotta win" talk.

Maybe the best thing the players did was watch some videos. The first showed highlights of some of the greatest soccer plays ever made. It was amazing—"awesome," as the players kept saying. But the next video showed soccer bloopers—all the stupid, awkward, sloppy plays that even great soccer players could make.

It was good for laughs, and it was something good to remember: Even the greatest players could mess up. And laugh.

★7★

Spring into Action

When the Pride walked out onto the field on Monday, anyone who had seen them play on Thursday would have thought that this was a different team. No one was talking about *not* messing up. Everyone was yelling back and forth about playing hard.

"Today's our day," Clayton yelled across the field. "I can feel it."

The Springers had some great players. They had won the championship the year before. And they had only lost one game so far this year. They didn't look excited. They looked sure of themselves, and calm.

A player named Robbie Jackson was the guy everyone in the whole league talked

about. He played forward, and he had all
the athletic skills plus some amazing moves.
Most teams tried to double-team him as
often as they could.

But Sterling Malone had the assignment
to mark him, and Sterling was one of the
best defenders in the league. He was very
fast, and he was in great shape. He had
proved before that he could stay with Jackson. Heidi knew he could do it again.

And she also felt that the Springers were
very "attack minded." They tended to score
a lot of goals, so they didn't worry if they
gave up a goal once in a while.

She had noticed something else, besides.
The fullbacks were the weakest part of the
Springers' team. Maybe she and Jacob could
get some open shots on them.

So Heidi went into the match with some
confidence, and so did her teammates.

Right from the opening kickoff, Angel
Park seemed to surprise the Springers with
the intense way they played defense. Their
transition from defense to attack was also
quick and fierce. They caught the Springers
off guard the first couple of times they took
over the ball.

The match had only been going a couple of minutes when Nate made a long punt upfield. Lian broke to the ball ahead of his defender. He used his quickness to push well into Springer territory, and then he rolled the ball off to Clayton. Clayton slowed as he saw the fullbacks in position ahead of him.

Clayton gave the impression that he was going to wait for more attackers to join him. Then, suddenly, he darted toward the goal area. The defending fullback tried to recover. He stuck out a leg and tried to reach for the ball. But all he got was Clayton's legs.

Clayton crashed to the ground, and the whistle blew.

The fullback was called for tripping in the goal area, and Clayton got a penalty shot.

He *drilled* it home!

The Pride was on top!

The whole team charged Clayton, and everyone slammed him on the back or slapped his hand.

Heidi liked what she saw.

The players weren't surprised, and they weren't hysterical with joy. They were happy and confident. This goal only proved what they believed.

They could beat these guys!

But things didn't go quite so easily after that. Both teams played extremely well—especially both defenses. The Springers' fullbacks were better than Heidi had thought. But then again, the Pride was better than the Springers had expected. Neither team could get the ball deep. Much of the game was being played in the middle of the field.

Clayton was everywhere.

And Henry was having his greatest game. He harassed his man constantly. He seemed to know exactly where the ball was going. He kept stepping in for the steal, or blocking off the Springers' wing from getting down the touchline.

Jackson was something to see—faking, cutting the ball back and forth, feinting and breaking, changing speeds. But Sterling was right there, and any Pride player who was close enough came over to double-team the guy.

Jackson was cool, and he was used to being doubled, but Heidi could see that he was getting frustrated. As the half was winding down and the Springers still hadn't scored, he started taking chances.

And finally it backfired on him.

Sterling was playing a little off Jackson most of the time. He was keeping his shoulders square, always staying between Jackson and the goal. He kept his eyes on the ball and ignored a lot of Jackson's fakes.

Then Jackson tried something once too often. He liked to turn his back on Sterling. He would fake to the left and at the same time drop the ball out to his right. Then he would break around to his right, pick up the ball, and try to get past Sterling.

He had made it work a couple of times, and only Sterling's quickness had prevented a good, clear shot.

But Sterling saw the fake coming this time. He saw Jackson turn and work his way to the right. He seemed to want Sterling a little to his left.

That was the tip-off. He had done the same thing every time he had made that move. So Sterling took the position Jackson wanted. But the instant Jackson made his fake, Sterling burst to the right and picked up the ball just as Jackson left it in the open.

The ball was right there waiting for Sterling!

It was perfect. Sterling was off and running. The Springers' fullbacks had pulled well upfield, and with Sterling's quickness, he was able to break into the clear.

Jackson recovered quickly, and he took off after Sterling. As he ran without the ball, he was able to get a one-step lead and move in to cut off Sterling.

But Heidi had also run hard. She was off to Sterling's right and close behind.

"I'm here, Sterling," she called.

Sterling suddenly pulled up and dropped the ball back to Heidi, who was moving fast. Jackson cut to her quickly, and now everyone on both teams was coming on hard, with Heidi in the lead.

Heidi knew she had to make something happen while the Pride still had the advantage. She angled a little outside the goal area, but she kept charging upfield, with Jackson running close.

That's when Jackson made his second mistake. He tried to get enough ahead of Heidi to cut in on her and take the ball away. As she saw him try that, she faked a short dribble kick. She then stepped to the side of the ball, turned back, and picked the ball up.

Jackson's momentum carried him forward, and she cut behind him and angled back toward the goal.

By now Clayton was in the goal area, but a defender was all over him. The goalie came out of the goal and charged straight at Heidi.

She adjusted her angle to the left, forcing the goalie to come to his right, and then she saw Clayton dart away from his defender.

She couldn't slow down enough to get a pass off, and Jackson was catching up fast.

Just then she heard Sterling. "Behind you, Heidi."

She suddenly slowed and let Jackson go by. She stopped, got control of the ball, and then dropped it off to Sterling just as he ran past her.

But Jackson had great reactions. He stopped quickly, and he cut to Sterling. Sterling couldn't drive to the goal, and he couldn't shoot. But he saw Clayton coming back toward him. He charged ahead, then he flipped the ball to his left, and Clayton had the ball.

The goalie was racing to get back in front of Clayton, and the fullback was charging him too. But Clayton saw a small opening, and he drove the ball at the net.

The goalie got a leg out and deflected the ball.

But not quite enough!

The ball popped into the corner of the net.

Goal!

Clayton jumped up and let out a wild cry of joy, and his teammates all leaped on him. Heidi had never seen them so happy. And she thought she knew why.

It was not just that they were ahead by two.

They were having fun.

And they were playing *so well.* That's what it was all about.

"Let's keep it going!" Clayton yelled. "Don't anybody—" But he stopped himself. "I mean—let's *stay after 'em.*"

And stay after them they did. The Pride played defense like a swarm of bees. They ran harder than the Springers, and when the ball got knocked away, they always got to it first.

And on attack they were thinking, helping each other, not trying to beat the Springers with their moves—but using quick, sharp passes.

The Springers looked overwhelmed. They didn't know what to do against players who went after them this hard and who never let up.

When halftime came, the score was still 2 to 0, and the Pride ran off the field while the Springers walked.

Heidi loved it. She had never had so much fun on a soccer field. But when she got to the sidelines, she heard the last thing she wanted to hear. Nate was saying, "We just *can't* let down now. We have to keep playing the way we've been playing."

And Clayton said, "Let's play the greatest defense of our lives."

Oh, no!

Sure, the team needed to keep playing hard and playing tough defense. But she heard a little of the nervousness, the fear, that she had heard from them in the last match.

★ 8 ★

Second Half

Coach Toscano joked with the players. He talked about having a victory party before every match.

But Heidi saw something happening.

Everyone was getting quiet now. She could almost hear them saying, "My gosh, we're ahead of the Springers at halftime—and we're shutting them out. This is too good to be true."

Coach Toscano told the players, "You have to keep after them, just the way you've been doing. They're worried right now. Usually they do to other teams what you did to them in the first half."

"Yeah, they're going to come out fighting

mad in the second half," Jared said. He tried to sound confident, but Heidi heard the little edge of fear in his voice.

She also felt a difference when she walked back out on the field to start the second half. The Springers were yelling and psyching each other up. They sounded excited, almost angry.

The Pride players were yelling too. But they didn't sound loose and happy the way they had in the beginning.

"All right, let's go get 'em!" she shouted. "Let's score, and put 'em down by three."

Clayton even said, "That's right!"

But Heidi could almost hear him saying, "But let's think mostly about defense."

It didn't take long to feel the difference in the play either. Now it was the Springers who were swarming on defense and staying tight on players, even when they didn't have the ball.

And Jackson had made up his mind to turn the match around. Nothing could have been more obvious.

Right after the half started, he dropped

back to the middle of the field, took a pass from Peter Metzger, the left wing, and then went after Sterling.

Sterling stayed tough. He didn't get faked out. But he gave enough ground so that Jackson could work his way up the field. But once Jackson got well into Pride territory, he cut past his own man to screen off Sterling.

Sterling saw the screen, and he slipped around the Springer player, but Jackson had bought himself some space.

He sprinted hard and then stopped, suddenly. He took a look at the goal, as though he wanted to shoot. Then he kicked a short pass back to Metzger.

Metzger came back toward Jackson, who was walking slowly with his hands on his hips.

And then, *bam*, Jackson cut behind Sterling and blasted toward the goal. Metzger led him perfectly, and Jackson took the pass in stride.

But Tammy switched off her mark and took Jackson, who tried to veer to his right to get a shot. Nate and Tammy had him blocked out well, and Heidi thought for just a moment that he was stopped.

But the guy had moves!

He cut the ball behind himself, spun, and broke to the left. He didn't have much of a window to the goal, since Nate was trying to recover and cut off Jackson's angle. But he took the little opening he had.

He slammed a left-footed shot at the corner. Nate dove, but he couldn't reach it. The shot got just inside the goalpost for the score.

Two to one, and the Springers were back in the game.

Now it was the Springers who celebrated. And now *they* were the ones sounding confident and happy.

"All right!" Jackson yelled to his teammates. "These guys can't stay with us for two halves. Let's put them away."

The Pride players had grown very quiet. Nate shouted, "Don't worry. Let's get another goal and make 'em take their words back."

None of the Pride players said much in response. Heidi watched the way they walked back upfield. She could tell they were afraid that the roof was about to cave in on them.

"Come on, Pride!" she shouted. "Let's get going again. Let's get all over them."

"Yeah!" Billy Bacon yelled. He had come into the game at fullback in place of Jared. "These guys think they're hot now. Let's shut 'em down again."

All the Pride picked up the cheer.

But Heidi didn't hear that loose, happy kind of confidence she had felt in the first half.

What she did see when the play started again, however, was that the team was going all out. The players were trying to do what they had to do. She could see that everyone was playing hard.

But it was the Springers who were giving even more. They were coming on fast, running hard, pushing the ball at the Pride. Heidi had to admit it. The Springers probably were a better team. Maybe no matter what Angel Park did they wouldn't be able to hold off Jackson and Metzger and some of the other Springer attackers.

Still, the defense stayed aggressive and

tough, and every time Blue Springs got close, someone on the Pride team came up with a big play.

Nate made three great stops, one of them on a ball that he had to dive for and knock away with his fist.

Lian made a fantastic steal. He came from behind just when Jackson appeared to have a good opening for a shot.

And Henry got a foot out and deflected a shot that Nate probably couldn't have stopped. Henry was still playing with all his heart.

The Pride players were getting off very few shots. They didn't come close to a score. It was beginning to appear as if their only hope was to keep playing tough defense and hold off the Springers' attack.

But the Springers weren't letting up, and once again it was Jackson who made something happen.

He took a rather long shot that Nate had no trouble handling. But when Nate tried to kick the ball out to the sideline to Trenton, Jackson doubled back and stole Nate's pass.

Both teams had started to run back upfield on the change of possession, and Jackson had a big advantage.

He dribbled straight at Nate.

Henry darted in between Jackson and the goal, but Metzger made a quick move back to the goal area, and Jackson saw him.

Jackson lifted the ball in the air for a header, but he got it up just a little too high. Metzger leaped, but he couldn't quite get it.

Sterling went for the ball, and everything seemed safe. But Jackson was there again. He took on Sterling in the goal area, and the two struggled for the ball.

When the ball suddenly popped out, it was Metzger who was closest, and he spun around and *blasted* the ball past Nate.

All their work was suddenly down the drain. The Angel Park players had played as hard as they possibly could, and now the game was all tied up, 2 to 2.

Not only that, but the Springers were flying high. They were jumping around and telling each other they still had plenty of time to put away another goal.

Clayton was losing it.

"I can't believe you did that," he shouted to Nate. "You have to watch for him to

double back like that. What were you thinking about? That's the one thing we couldn't
do—just *give* them a goal—after all the work
we've done to build up a lead."

"Clayton, I *know!*" Nate said. "I messed
up, okay?"

Heidi knew Nate was furious with himself.

"Hey, you guys," Heidi shouted. "This
match isn't over. We can score again."

"Yeah, right!" Clayton said. "They aren't
going to let up now."

Heidi walked up close to Clayton and
looked him in the eye. "Clayton, you're a
great player, but you've got a loser's attitude. We made up our minds that we were
going to have fun today and play our best.
Now you're right back to all the negative
stuff."

"Well, who's right? You guys are the los-
ers. I just wish once in my life I could play
for a team like the Springers."

It was the worst thing he could have said.
Most of the players on the Pride team heard
it—and so did some of the Springers.

And, of course, the Springers jumped
right on it. They were soon yelling, "Hey,

Lindsay wants to play for us. Too bad he's not good enough to make our team!"

Heidi knew Clayton was sorry he had said it, but he was also too proud to say so. He walked back upfield for the kickoff.

The Pride players were *angry*. They had had about enough of this kind of stuff from Clayton. "Let the jerk go play for someone else!" Brian said. "He's not as good as he thinks he is anyway."

"No one's as good as *he* thinks *he* is!" Tammy said.

"He was just mad," Heidi said. "He didn't mean it."

But none of the other players were that quick to let it go. Heidi heard a lot more mumbling about Clayton as the players walked back up the field.

Heidi knew things couldn't be worse. The Pride players looked as though they had already lost, and the Springers seemed to think it was just a matter of time before they scored again.

Somehow Heidi had to do something. She had to get that other Pride team back—the one that had played the first half.

And she had to do it right now.

★9★

Up for Grabs

Suddenly Heidi yelled, "Just a minute, ref! Hold up." Then she waved her arms and shouted, "Everyone over here. Hurry!"

All the Angel Park players trotted over to her even though the referee was saying, "You can't do that. It's time to play."

"Just a second. This is an emergency."

The referee didn't ever give Heidi permission, but she soon had the whole team gathered around her. "Look, you guys," she said very seriously as she looked around at them, "don't say anything about Jackson's little problem. We don't want to embarrass him."

All the players looked confused. Heidi

kept looking around at them. Finally Clayton said, "Heidi, what are you talking about?" He sounded annoyed.

"I know he looks funny, but don't say anything. We want to be good sports."

The referee was shouting that he was going to let the Springers kick off whether Angel Park was ready or not. Some of the Springers were shouting insults.

"Heidi, what in the heck are you talking about?" Nate asked.

"That stupid look, of course."

"Heidi, lay off," Sterling said. "We gotta play."

But some of the players were turning to take a look at Jackson.

The referee was setting the ball down, and a few of the players were getting frantic.

"Come on, Heidi!" Clayton said. "Let's go."

"See, the problem is, he thinks he's going to win. So that's why he has that goofy look on his face. And I just can't help feeling sorry for him. So go ahead and celebrate, but don't rub it in, okay? He would feel terrible if he knew what we're about to do to him."

"*Yeah!*" Billy shouted. "Let's do it!"

"No, Billy," Heidi whispered. "Be quiet about it. Let's all just pat each other on the back and say, 'Way to go.' But don't jump up and down and scream and everything."

Coach Toscano was yelling now. "Get to your positions, kids. Come on!"

Heidi thought she had blown it. Billy was about the only one who seemed—

And then Nate started to laugh. "That's right!" he said. "Way to go, team. We're about to *flatten* those guys! Congratulations!"

The players suddenly began to shout and pat each other on the back.

"*Yeah!*" Sterling yelled. "We're going to chew 'em up and spit 'em out!"

Heidi was watching Clayton. He didn't say a word for a long time. He looked ready to tell the other players not to act so stupid. But then he seemed to make a decision.

"We've got these clowns!" he said. "They don't have a chance!"

It was exactly what the team needed.

All the players cheered and then ran to their positions. Everyone was laughing and shouting, and Billy yelled, "Hey, Jackson, don't feel bad. Everyone has to lose sooner or later. It just happens to be your turn today."

Jackson yelled back, "Do I look worried?"

But Heidi thought maybe he did. The Springers seemed to be aware that something had changed in the Pride. The Blue Springs players had stopped yelling. Maybe they remembered how the Pride had played in the first half.

Maybe they were a little worried that the first-half team was back.

And it didn't take long to find out that that was the case.

The Pride went on defense like a pack of wolves. They were everywhere, working hard, snapping at the heels of the Springers. And the Springers seemed a little rattled.

When the Pride went on attack, they were pushing, looking to make things happen.

A couple of times they came close to scoring. They got off some strong shots. But the Springers' goalie was tough, and he made some good stops. This Springer team was a little back on its heels, but the players were fighters, and they weren't about to let Angel Park get anything cheap.

Gradually, time was running down.

The Pride was working frantically, and they were keeping pressure on the Blue Springs defense. They just couldn't get the goal that they needed.

But then Clayton tackled a Springer midfielder and took the ball away. Chris yelled, "*Attack!*" and the team took off up the field.

"Let's do it!" Heidi yelled. As she ran alongside Clayton, he slowed and rolled an easy pass to her. At the same time, he burst past his defender, and Heidi led him on a perfect wall pass—the old give-and-go play.

Clayton saw his opening and raced toward the goal area, where a fullback came out to meet him.

Heidi could see that the Pride had a four-on-three advantage. Chris was to her left and Jacob was just outside the goal area on the right. She ran away from Clayton, who was in the middle, so that the three defenders had to spread themselves to cover all the angles.

The last couple of times Clayton had gotten a chance to drive into the middle he had taken the shot himself. This time he made it look as though he wanted to do the same thing.

He slowed and eyed the goal. Instead of shooting, however, he knocked the ball off to his right as Jacob dashed into the center. But a fullback managed to get in the way. Jacob got control of the ball, but he lost his chance to shoot.

The defense was falling back now, and the advantage was being lost. Something had to happen fast.

Heidi knew she and Chris were both on the left side with only one fullback, so she ran toward the defender and then cut to the right, pulling the guy with her.

She knew Chris would be open now. She hoped Jacob could get the ball across to him.

But the fullback saw the same thing and made a quick decision to go back to cover Chris. Suddenly it was Heidi and Clayton who had a defender two-on-one.

Jacob spun and kicked the ball toward Clayton, but the defender stepped in and tried to clear the ball. He got a foot in the way, and the ball deflected and rolled free.

Clayton pounced on it and dropped it straight back behind him.

Straight to Heidi.

She took a quick step to control the ball, and then she spun and fired.

But the goalie guessed right and dove in front of the ball.

The ball bounced in the air and came down to one of the fullbacks.

The chance was lost. The fullback kicked . . .

No! The fullback tried to clear the ball, but Chris stepped in and kicked the ball loose. It rolled toward Heidi, and she trapped it.

This time she spun and faked the kick. And the goalie dove.

Once he was on the ground, all she had to do was give it a little punch. The ball rolled behind the goalie and into the net.

Score!

It took Heidi a few seconds to believe that

the Pride was on top again, 3 to 2. By then Clayton was hugging her as if she were his oldest friend.

"You did it! You did it! We've got 'em now!" he yelled.

The whole team soon mobbed her.

By the time they were running back downfield again, she had finally told herself it was real. She leaped in the air with both fists raised and shouted, *"Yeah!"*

Jared, standing on the sidelines, yelled, "Okay, everyone. There's less than two minutes to go. You've got to play tough defense. Don't let—"

But it was Clayton who yelled, "No. Forget that. Let's go after 'em and stay after 'em. Let's score again."

As it turned out, they didn't score, but they kept the pressure on, and Jacob took a shot that had a chance. The Springers should have been the team putting on the pressure, but they seemed overwhelmed. The Pride was just too much for them today.

And when the game was over, what happened next was sort of strange. The Pride had done their celebrating ahead of time. They didn't go nearly as crazy as Heidi had thought they might.

Everyone seemed happy and satisfied but not really surprised.

The Springers were standing around looking stunned. They were talking quietly, and Heidi had the feeling they were saying, "Where did *they* come from? This is not the team we expected."

Coach Toscano called the kids together, and they all sat down on the grass. "We can still win the championship!" Sterling yelled, and everyone cheered.

The coach told the kids, "Yes, we can. But let's play one game at a time. This is what soccer is all about. This is fun. From now on, we don't worry—we just *play* with all our hearts."

When the coach finished talking, Heidi lay back on the grass and let the nice warm sun bake into her face. She just wanted to savor the feeling for a little while. She could hear all the happy voices around her, and she felt great inside.

But then a shadow covered her eyes, and

she looked up to see who it was. Clayton
was standing over her. "Would you like to
go get some ice cream or something? My
father's buying."

"Is everyone going?"

"Sure. It's a celebration party."

"We already had that, remember?"

"Yeah, I know. I'm not talking about this
game. We're going to go celebrate the next
one."

"All right!" Heidi said, and she jumped up.
"But if we keep this up, what are we going
to do when we win the championship?"

Clayton thought about that for a moment
and then said, "Well, we could have a victory party for next season."

Heidi liked that. She was about to run to
tell her parents where she was going, but
Clayton stopped her. *"You* won this game
for us, Heidi," he said.

"Not really. The ball just bounced to me
at the right time. Chris is the one who kept
it alive."

"That's not what I'm talking about and
you know it. I almost ruined everything.
Telling everyone I wanted to play for the

Springers—that was stupid. But then you turned everything around."

"Let's forget about all that. Let's just be happy we won."

Heidi did feel pretty good about what she had done. She just didn't want to talk about it.

"Come on. Let's go celebrate," she said. "Now that we've got this team all backward and upside down, we've got to keep it that way."

League Standings

Kickers	5–1
Springers	4–2
Pride	4–2
Tornadoes	3–3
Racers	3–3
Bandits	1–5
Gila Monsters	1–5

Match 5 Scores:

Pride	1	Gila Monsters	0
Springers	5	Racers	2
Tornadoes	3	Kickers	1
Bandits	bye		

Match 6 Scores:

Racers	2	Pride	1
Springers	7	Bandits	4
Kickers	5	Gila Monsters	1
Tornadoes	bye		

Match 7 Scores:

Pride	3	Springers	2
Kickers	4	Bandits	3
Tornadoes	8	Gila Monsters	2
Racers	bye		

Kickoff

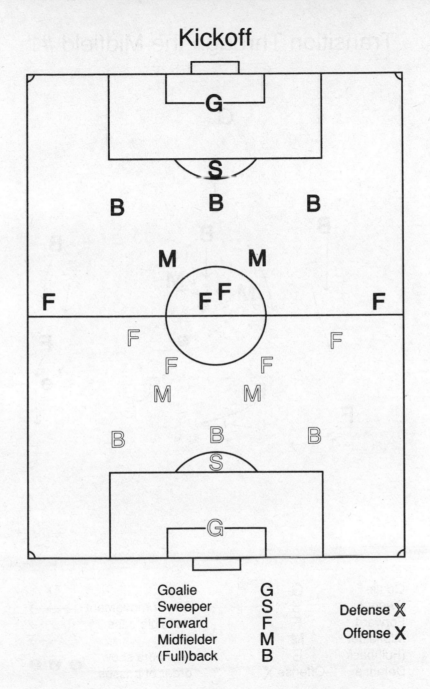

Goalie	**G**
Sweeper	**S**
Forward	**F**
Midfielder	**M**
(Full)back	**B**

Defense X
Offense X

Transition Through the Midfield #1

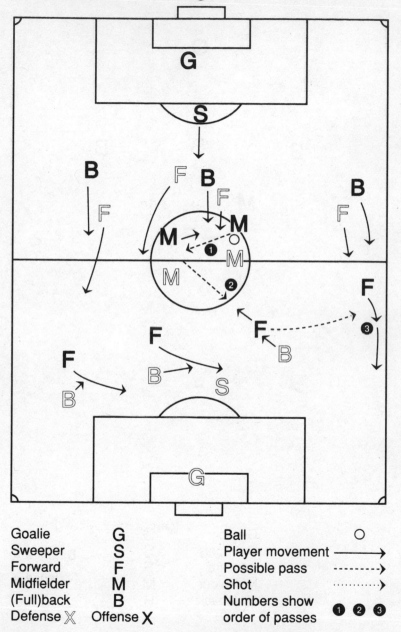

Goalie	**G**	Ball	○
Sweeper	**S**	Player movement	—→
Forward	**F**	Possible pass	------→
Midfielder	**M**	Shot	·······→
(Full)back	**B**	Numbers show	❶ ❷ ❸
Defense X	Offense **X**	order of passes	

96

Throw-in #1

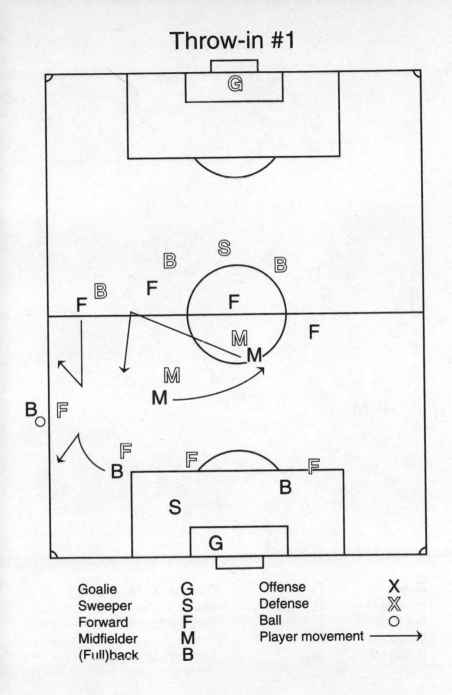

Goalie	G	Offense	X
Sweeper	S	Defense	X
Forward	F	Ball	O
Midfielder	M	Player movement	——→
(Full)back	B		

Throw-in #2

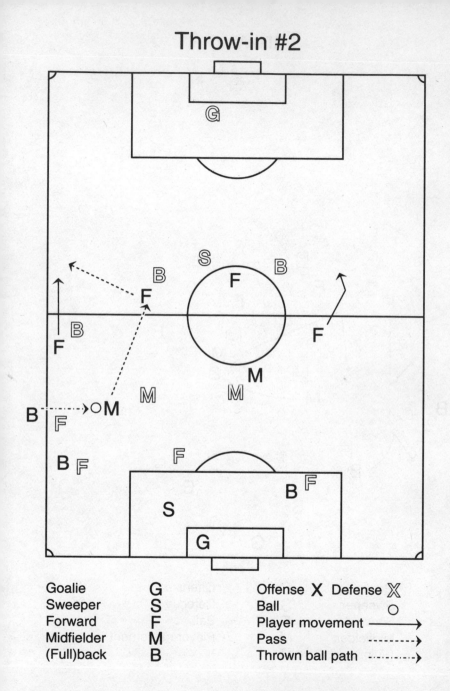

Goalie	**G**	Offense **X** Defense X
Sweeper	**S**	Ball ○
Forward	**F**	Player movement ——→
Midfielder	**M**	Pass ------→
(Full)back	**B**	Thrown ball path —·—·→

Direct Kick—Outside Penalty Area

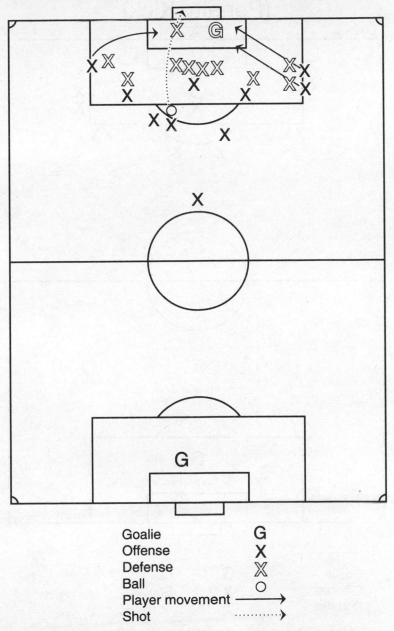

Goalie G

Offense X

Defense X̷

Ball ○

Player movement ——→

Shot ·········►

Direct Kick—Inside Penalty Box
(Penalty Kick)

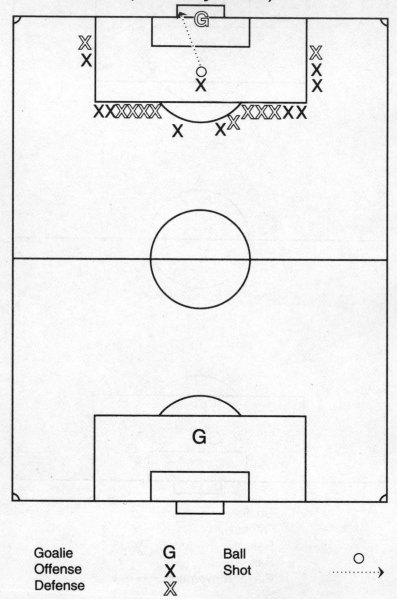

Goalie	**G**	Ball
Offense	**X**	Shot
Defense	**X**	

Note: The goalie must stand on the end line and cannot move until the ball is kicked.

Glossary

corner kick A free kick taken from a corner area by a member of the attacking team, after the defending team has propelled the ball out-of-bounds across the goal line.

cover A defensive maneuver in which a player places himself between an opponent and the goal.

cross pass A pass across the field, often toward the center, intended to set up the shooter.

cutting Suddenly changing directions while dribbling the ball in order to deceive a defender.

direct free kick An unimpeded shot at the goal, awarded to a team sustaining a major foul.

dribbling Maneuvering the ball at close range with only the feet.

feinting Faking out an opponent with deceptive moves.

forwards Players whose primary purpose is to score goals. Also referred to as "strikers."

free kick A direct *or* indirect kick awarded to a team, depending on the type of foul committed by the opposing team.

fullbacks Defensive players whose main purpose is to keep the ball out of the goal area.

goalkeeper The ultimate defender against attacks on the goal, and the only player allowed to use his hands.

halfbacks See Midfielders.

heading Propelling the ball with the head, especially the forehead.

indirect free kick A shot at the goal involving at least two players, awarded to a team sustaining a minor foul.

juggling A drill using the thighs, feet, ankles, or head to keep the ball in the air continuously.

kickoff A center place kick which starts the action at the beginning of both the first and second halves or after a goal has been scored.

marking Guarding a particular opponent.

midfielders Players whose main purpose is to get the ball from the defensive players to the forwards. Also called "halfbacks."

penalty kick A direct free kick awarded to a member of the attacking team from a spot 12 yards in front of the goal. All other players must stay outside the penalty area except for the goalie, who must remain stationary until the ball is in play.

punt   A drop kick made by the goalkeeper.

shooting   Making an attempt to score a goal.

strikers   See Forwards.

sweeper   The last player, besides the goalkeeper, to defend the goal against attack.

tackling   Stealing the ball from an opponent by using the feet or a shoulder charge.

total soccer   A system by which players are constantly shifting positions as the team shifts from offense to defense. Also called "positionless soccer."

volley kick   A kick made while the ball is still in the air.

wall   A defensive barrier of players who stand in front of the goal area to aid the goalkeeper against free kicks.

wall pass   This play involves a short pass from one teammate to another, followed by a return pass to the first player as he runs past the defender. Also called the "give-and-go."

wingbacks   Outside fullbacks.

wingers   Outside forwards.

DEAN HUGHES has written many books for children, including the popular *Nutty* stories and *Jelly's Circus*. He has also published such works of literary fiction for young adults as the highly acclaimed *Family Pose*. Writing keeps Mr. Hughes very busy, but he does find time to run and play golf—and he loves to watch almost all sports. His home is in Utah. He and his wife have three children, all in college.

It's going to take teamwork...

ANGEL PARK SOCCER STARS #2

Defense!
by Dean Hughes

The preseason soccer tournament is starting, and it's time
for the Angel Park Pride to find out what they're made of.
Their coach keeps telling them to have fun, but Nate
Matheson, the team's goalie, takes it a bit more seriously.
So when he sees his teammates making dumb mistakes,
he loses his temper. But he soon realizes that the only way
the team is going to win any games is if he stops yelling and
starts leading. The only question is, how can Nate get his
teammates to listen if they're all mad at him?

FIRST TIME IN PRINT!

A BULLSEYE BOOK PUBLISHED BY ALFRED A. KNOPF, INC.

Play ball with the kids from Angel Park!

ANGEL PARK ALL-STARS™

by Dean Hughes

Meet Kenny, Harlan, and Jacob—three talented young players
on Angel Park's Little League team. They're in for plenty of
fastball action...as well as fun and friendship. Collect them
all! Watch for new titles and new sports coming soon!

 - ✂

Available wherever books are sold, or use this coupon.

_____	679-80426-9	#1	**Making the Team**	$2.95
_____	679-80427-7	#2	**Big Base Hit**	$2.95
_____	679-80428-5	#3	**Winning Streak**	$2.95
_____	679-80429-3	#4	**What a Catch!**	$2.95
_____	679-80430-7	#5	**Rookie Star**	$2.95
_____	679-80431-5	#6	**Pressure Play**	$2.95
_____	679-80432-3	#7	**Line Drive**	$2.95
_____	679-80433-1	#8	**Championship Game**	$2.95
_____	679-81536-8	#9	**Superstar Team**	$2.95
_____	679-81537-6	#10	**Stroke of Luck**	$2.95
_____	679-81538-4	#11	**Safe at First**	$2.95
_____	679-81539-2	#12	**Up to Bat**	$2.95
_____	679-81540-6	#13	**Play-off**	$2.95
_____	679-81541-4	#14	**All Together Now**	$2.95

Alfred A. Knopf, Inc., P.O. Box 100, Westminster, MD 21157
Please send me the books I have checked above. I am enclosing
$_____ .
(Please add $2.00 for shipping and handling for the first book and 50¢
for each additional book.) Send check or money order—no cash or
C.O.D.'s please. Prices are subject to change without notice. Valid in
U.S. only. All orders are subject to availability of books.
Name _____
Address _____
City _____ State _____ Zip _____

Please allow at least 4 weeks for delivery.   APAS 1